BASKETBALL

by
Jane Duden
and
Susan Osberg

CRESTWOOD HOUSE
New York

Maxwell Macmillan Canada
Toronto

Maxwell Macmillan International
New York Oxford Singapore Sydney

Library of Congress Cataloging-in-Publication Data
Duden, Jane.
  Basketball / by Jane Duden and Susan Osberg.—1st ed.
    p. cm. — (Sportslines)
  Summary: A collection of facts, trivia, and statistics about the popular sport of
basketball.
  ISBN 0-89686-627-0
  1. Basketball—United States—History—Juvenile literature. [1. Basketball—History.
2. Basketball—Miscellanea.] I. Osberg, Susan. II. Title. III. Series.
GV885.7.D83   1991
796.323′0973—dc20   90-28515
                                                    CIP
                                                    AC

Photo Credits
AP—Wide World Photos: 4, 13, 14, 17, 18, 19, 21, 22, 24, 25, 27, 28, 30, 31, 33, 35, 37,
39, 41
Naismith Memorial Basketball Hall of Fame: 7, 8, 10, 11, 16
Texas Christian University: 34

Macmillan Publishing Company   Maxwell Macmillan Canada, Inc.
866 Third Avenue   1200 Eglinton Avenue East
New York, NY 10022   Suite 200
                                 Don Mills, Ontario M3C 3N1

CRESTWOOD HOUSE

Macmillan Publishing Company is part of the Maxwell Communication Group of Companies.

Produced by Flying Fish Studio

Printed in the United States of America

First edition

10 9 8 7 6 5 4 3 2 1

Contents

Inside Basketball

Basketball has come a long way. From its ragtag beginnings in the 1890s, it has grown up. Each era brings new superstars. Today we see new heights in the game's players, scores and records. Court thrills, spills and skills are better than ever. Fans ask: What teams are the best? Who are the favorite players? Read on for a view from the top.

A Peachy New Game

They complained about another winter of boring exercises in gym class. The students at the YMCA Training School in Springfield, Massachusetts, wanted a new indoor game to play. So their gym teacher, James A. Naismith, invented one! Naismith drew up a list of 13 rules. He asked the school janitor to nail peach baskets to the balcony railings at both ends of the gym. Two teams of nine men were called together. He handed them a soccer ball and showed them the baskets. The first basketball game took place on December 21, 1891. What happened when the ball went into the peach basket? A man hauled a ladder onto the court. Then he climbed the ladder and took the ball out of the basket. (The janitor hadn't cut the bottoms out of the peach baskets!)

James A. Naismith, the inventor of basketball

Basketball caught on quickly. Many of Naismith's students became athletic directors in YMCAs across the country. The game of basketball went with them. Within five years, it was being played in schools and colleges everywhere. And what of the teacher, James Naismith? The inventor of basketball became a doctor of medicine. When the Basketball Hall of Fame was opened in 1959, Dr. Naismith was its first honoree. He had done something no one else had ever done: He invented the only major sport that is completely American. The Naismith Memorial Basketball Hall of Fame was named after him.

Buffalo Stampede

Almost as soon as basketball was invented, men joined together to form teams. The Buffalo (New York) Germans was one of the earliest. It was organized by the YMCA in 1895. The players started as an unpaid team of 14-year-old boys. Over the next 20 years their fame grew. In that time they put together a 792-86 record. They also had a 111-game winning streak! With that kind of reputation, the team drew crowds. They became the first pros to command big money. The Germans were considered the best basketball team of the first decade of the 20th century. Their record earned the team a place in the Hall of Fame.

Pay for Play

Basketball was a play-without-pay sport until 1896. Professional basketball came about when the players themselves had to pay to play. It started when some local YMCAs banned

The Buffalo Germans

basketball in their gyms. They claimed that too much space was being wasted on only 10 or 20 men playing at one time. One Trenton, New Jersey, team went scouting for somewhere else to play. They rented the auditorium of the downtown Masonic lodge for $25. To pay the rent, they charged admission. After the game, they had a hatful of money. It paid the rent and more. The extra money went to the players. Professional basketball was born! Fifteen dollars was the whopping salary for each player that night!

Now players negotiate million-dollar contracts for their talents. At this writing, the highest paid player for the National Basketball Association (NBA) is John "Hot Rod" Williams, center/forward for Miami Heat. He will earn $28 million over seven years!

7

Small Wonders

One of basketball's great performers was Barney Sedran. He was only 5 feet 4 and weighed 118 pounds. In Barney's day, players often switched leagues and teams from one night to another. They did that to make more money. Barney scored 17 baskets in one game, shooting at a hoop without a backboard. He led his Carbondale, Pennsylvania, team to 35 straight wins in the Tri County League. But that's not all! In that same season, Barney played a complete schedule with the Utica team of the New York State League! Barney played from 1912 to 1926. He was elected to the Basketball Hall of Fame in 1962.

Barney Sedran

Today Spud Webb proves that short guys can dunk the ball too. Playing for the Atlanta Hawks, Spud wins slam-dunk contests at a mere 5 feet 7.

Famous Flakes

Since 1924 kids have been Wheaties watchers. They want to see who eats the "breakfast of champions." Since Wheaties came out in 1924, only seven athletes have appeared on the front of the Wheaties cereal box. Who are they? Bob Richards (1956-70), Bruce Jenner (1977-79), Mary Lou Retton (1984-86), Pete Rose (1985-86), Walter Payton (1986-88), Chris Evert (1987) and basketball's Michael Jordan (1989-90).

The Original Celtics

A team called the Celtics (no connection to today's Boston team) ruled the game of basketball during the 1920s. The team was organized as the New York Celtics in 1914. It was disbanded during World War I. After the war the team was reorganized, taking the name of Original Celtics. They changed the game of basketball, on and off the court.

When the Celtics were not playing in New York, they barnstormed. They traveled around the country and made money by playing against local teams. They were the first team to do away with man-to-man defense. They were first to use defensive switching. They invented the pivot play. The team broke up during the Depression. But the Original Celtics did so much to develop basketball that they were awarded a place in the Hall of Fame.

The Unbeatable Rens

In the early days of basketball, black athletes played on all-black teams in all-black leagues. Only in exhibition matches did the black and white teams play against one another. The New York Rens, started in 1922, was a black team from Harlem. By the thirties, they were on top and famous. From 1932 to 1936, the Rens had compiled 473 wins, with only 49 losses. That included an 88-game winning streak. The great New York Rens were inducted as a team into the Basketball Hall of Fame in 1963.

The New York Rens

Naismith Memorial Hall of Fame

The Basketball Hall of Fame

By the 1940s basketball was a major American sport. High schools and colleges all over the United States had teams. Basketball had become an Olympic sport in 1936. What could be done so that basketball's greatest stars would not be forgotten?

Plans were begun in the late 1940s for a basketball hall of fame. The National Association of Basketball Coaches got the ball rolling. They decided to locate the memorial in Springfield, Massachusetts. That is where the game was invented.

The Hall of Fame came into being in 1959. Unlike most sports halls of fame, the Basketball Hall of Fame honors persons from all levels of the game. It honors great players and great coaches. It also honors writers, officials and others who have made a lasting mark on the game. To be eligible, a

11

player or an official must have been retired for 5 years. A coach must have had 25 years of coaching experience. Among the original honorees were James Naismith and the first team to play the game—the 18 students in Naismith's 1891 YMCA class.

The Basketball Hall of Fame museum was opened in 1968. Some of the museum's exhibits are unusual. On display is a basketball that was dribbled 225 miles and another that was kept in play for 206 hours. And Detroit Piston Bob Lanier's size-20 sneakers are there too. How many could fill those shoes?

The NBA's First Big Star

At 6 feet 10, George Mikan was basketball's first big man. In 1945, he led De Paul University to a major college title—mostly by hanging out by the hoop. He'd hop up, then drop the ball in. Dunking had become a dangerous scoring threat.

These days Mikan's name may not be included among the greatest basketball centers. But he was the NBA's first big star. George Mikan was such a dominant player that people called him a one-man gang. On December 13, 1949, the marquee outside Madison Square Garden read: GEO MIKAN VS. KNICKS. Mikan joined the Minneapolis Lakers in 1947. With Mikan at center, the Lakers won championships six of their first seven seasons.

A basketball Hall of Famer, Mikan retired in 1954 at age 29. But fans wrote Mikan many letters urging him to return. He did. He played the last half of the 1955-56 season. He retired for good in 1958.

Ed (*left*) and George (*right*) Mikan leap for a high push.

George Mikan, the Babe Ruth of basketball, still remembers his rocky road to greatness. "I started wearing glasses when I was 12," he says. "People told me that anyone who wore glasses could never be a great athlete. And I always took a lot of taunts because I was so big. In college they laughed and said I'd trip over the foul line." Well, George Mikan showed them all.

Bob Cousy

"Mr. Basketball"

He was one of the most spectacular players basketball has ever known. He could outdodge, outrun and outshoot anyone on the court, earning him the nickname "Mr. Basketball." That player was Bob Cousy. By the time Bob had graduated from Holy Cross College in 1950, he had been an All-American twice and the team's Most Valuable Player (MVP). Then Bob Cousy joined the Boston Celtics, a losing team since their start in 1946. Cousy helped put them on the basketball map. He led that team to six world championships. The Celtics were the leaders in the NBA for over a decade.

Cousy was a ball-handling genius. He was a master of the "fast break" that made the Celtics famous. He once dribbled single-handedly for the final 23 seconds of a game against the New York Knicks to ensure a one-point Celtics victory. Cousy averaged 18.5 points per game over his 13-year career. Robert J. Cousy—the Cooz—became a Basketball Hall of Famer in 1970.

Foul Play

The referee's whistle almost overheated. This was one basketball game that saw almost as many fouls as points. It took place on New Year's Day 1954. Grafton downed Weston, 61-55. But the two West Virginia teams set a national high school record with 110 fouls. Weston committed 59 and Grafton 51. What a way to foul up the New Year!

In the Nick of Time

Twenty-four seconds to shoot—no more. The 24-second clock came along just in the nick of time. Pro basketball fans had grown frustrated by the stalling tactics of the day. Teams were choosing to stall earlier and earlier in the game, especially if they were the underdogs. On November 22, 1950, the Fort Wayne Pistons held the basketball for most of the game to defeat the Minneapolis Lakers, 19-18. The crowd was enraged.

Players hated it too. Bob Cousy was good at dribbling out the clock. He was so good that—out of frustration—Paul Hoffman of the Baltimore Bullets once tackled him.

Danny Biasone, owner of the Syracuse Nationals, was the man who dreamed up the 24-second clock. How did he get the idea? He explained: "I figured if the teams combined for 120 shots in a game and the game was 48 minutes long...I divided

120 shots into 2,880 seconds, I believe. The answer was 24." Owners liked the idea and agreed to try the rule. It was adopted for the 1954-55 regular season. Now the 24-second clock is the heartbeat of the game.

Up in Smoke

Red Auerbach was his name. He was the only coach in NBA history to win over a thousand games. That made him the winningest coach in pro basketball. Under Auerbach the Boston Celtics won nine NBA championships. Auerbach developed great players like Bob Cousy, Bill Russell and John Havlicek.

Red Auerbach wasn't always popular with the opposition. His on-court antics cost him $17,000 in fines over his career. But Celtics fans loved him. They learned to watch for his cigars. Auerbach didn't smoke for most of the game. But toward the end, when he was sure of a Celtics win, he would light up. It was a sign that sent Celtics fans wild. And that cigar was a sure insult to the other team, whose win was going up in smoke.

Red Auerbach

16

Bill Russell leaps for a basket.

Basketball Thief

The year was 1956. At $19,500, Bill Russell was an expensive rookie for the Boston Celtics. After the first six games, Bill nearly gave back the money and quit. He felt he was the worst shooter in the NBA. Bill recalled, "I got pushed, pulled, pinched, punched, bumped and stepped on because I was too clumsy to get out of the way." But his coach believed in him. He told Bill to forget about making points and just get the ball. After all, a player can't shoot if he doesn't have the ball.

That's what Bill did. Bill Russell gave new meaning to the game of keep-away. He became the hottest shot blocker around. At 6 feet 9, Bill had arms and legs like an octopus. Rebounding, blocking, and in-your-face rejects were his game. Offensively, he keyed the fast break with long passes downcourt where other Celtics players waited, ready to score. In his new approach to the game, Russell changed the way it was played. He earned the nickname the Destroyer. In his rookie year, Bill made a record 49 rebounds in one game. The Celtics won the NBA title that year. In 1958-59, Bill Russell helped put the Celtics on a roll. They won eight championships in a row.

17

He Floats, He Flies

Was he the greatest forward ever to play basketball? Thousands of fans thought so. They came to watch Elgin Baylor take flight. His records were astounding. In 1959 he was Rookie of the Year. He led his Minneapolis (later Los Angeles) Lakers in scoring. He was the first team All-Star that year and for the next nine. In his 13-year career, Elgin Baylor piled up 23,149 points in 846 regular-season games.

Baylor appeared to defy the laws of gravity. He could float, soar and hang in midair. Former Laker Hot Rod Hundley put it this way: "My biggest thrill came the night Elgin Baylor and I combined for 73 points in Madison Square Garden. Elgin had 71 of them."

Elgin Baylor takes flight.

Slam and Jam

In 1960 Bill Russell and Wilt Chamberlain came face-to-face. Basketball's defensive genius met the game's offensive giant. Needless to say, these two players were big rivals! Wilt stood on tiptoe and stuffed the ball into the basket. Bill blocked, stole and ran. The Boston Celtics beat the Philadelphia Warriors four games to two in playoffs. It was the first of many head-to-head battles between Russell and Chamberlain. Fans loved it!

Wilt Chamberlain

The Chocolate Factory

Wilt Chamberlain's sweetest drops came in a town best known for Hershey's chocolate. Chamberlain's Philadelphia Warriors were playing the New York Knickerbockers on March 2, 1962, in Hershey, Pennsylvania. The fans were hungry. They knew that Wilt had broken all scoring records during the year. The scoring record for one game was 78 points. It was a mark already held by Chamberlain. Could he beat his own record? Crowds followed every move. Chamberlain dropped baskets as easy as gum drops. With only 46 seconds left, Wilt made his last shot. That basket gave him an incredible 100 points for the game! Fans will drool over that moment forever.

19

Second to None

UCLA coach John Wooden had a record unequaled in the history of college basketball. He won more NCAA (National Collegiate Athletic Association) titles than any other coach. Ever. Anywhere. How did he do it? He did not scream insults at his players. Instead he taught basketball as if it were a religion. Kareem Abdul-Jabbar's mother described Wooden as "more like a minister than a coach." Wooden would speak softly but firmly to his players. He often reminded them, "You are here for an education. That comes first. Basketball comes second." Over a 12-season span (1964 to 1975) Wooden led UCLA to ten championships.

An Awesome Record

In 1966 famed Celtics coach Red Auerbach retired. Bill Russell was named to replace him. He became the first black to coach an American League professional team. Russell was a player-coach for three seasons. The Celtics had three winning seasons under Russell. In 1966-67, they finished with 60 wins and 21 losses. In 1967-68 their record was 54-28. In 1968-69 the Celtics season was 48-34. And the Celtics won the NBA championship in 1968 and 1969. Russell ended his playing career with an awesome 21,721 rebounds. He said it himself: "I just don't know how to lose."

Trick-Shot Champion

The trick-shot artist of all time was Wilfred Hetzel. In 1970 Wilfred started giving basketball shows for girls and boys. He would do anything to get the ball into the basket. He would

Trick shot master
Wilfred Hetzel

shoot it. Kick it. Bounce it. Some of his most amazing shots:

144 foul shots without a miss—standing on one foot.

35 shots bounced in without a miss.

92 out of 100 foul shots—standing on one foot and blind-folded.

3 basketball dropkicks in a row—while 20 feet away.

How close can you come to Wilfred's record? By the way, he was 60 years old!

Guess Who?

An interview with Wilt Chamberlain:

Q. Did you ever use a disguise to avoid being recognized?

A. Yes, my sunglasses.

Q. Did they work?

A. Would they work on an elephant?

Kareem
Abdul-Jabbar
(*right*) leaps
for a
skyhook.

Kareem of the Crop

One of the most exciting players ever to walk onto a basketball court was Kareem Abdul-Jabbar. He was famous at a younger age and for a longer time than anyone else in the sport. He became one of the most famous athletes in the world. Kareem Abdul-Jabbar glowered at and towered over the basketball world. At 7 feet 2, this giant was one of the first basketball players to dominate on both offense and defense. Born Lew Alcindor, he became an instant star at UCLA. He scored 56 points in his first varsity game. In his junior year,

Alcindor embraced the Islamic faith. Later, in 1971, he changed his name to Kareem Abdul-Jabbar. The name means "generous, powerful servant of Allah." Powerful? You bet. Kareem changed the face of college basketball. Rules were rewritten to size down the giant's natural ability. In 1967 the NCAA outlawed the dunk shot, Abdul-Jabbar's favorite. That didn't stop him. He polished his famous skyhook, discovered when he was nine years old. After UCLA, Abdul-Jabbar went on to lead the Milwaukee Bucks out of the cellar to an NBA title in two seasons. He later starred with the Los Angeles Lakers. Kareem Abdul-Jabbar retired after a 20-year playing career. He was voted the Most Valuable Player a record six times. In 1971 and again in 1985, he was the MVP in the championship playoff series. That says a lot for his long-lasting skill and his perfect shot! His playing days are over but his feats are still recalled.

Equal Opportunity

At first girls were allowed to play basketball only when boys weren't using the courts. They used a half-court style of play, since females were thought too weak to run the full court. Most schools did not offer any sports teams for girls, claiming they didn't have the space, money or coaches. In 1972 the U.S. Congress passed a law known as Title Nine. The new law required most schools to offer equal opportunities to boys and girls. Schools started teams for girls, and colleges began awarding athletic scholarships to girls. Today girls can choose from among many sports.

Women's Basketball

Women's basketball has grown in popularity. Players like Theresa Shank Grentz, basketball's first "big woman," have helped make it an exciting game of skill and competition. Theresa stood all of 5 feet 11. But she led her small school, Immaculata College, to three national titles in the 1970s. She went on to coach women's basketball at Rutgers. Then Lusia Harris Stewart came on the basketball scene. At 6 feet 3, she was closer to the hoops by 4 inches than Grentz. As center she scored the first basket at the Montreal Olympics in 1976. Small but mighty Debbie Brock was one of the shortest guards who ever played. At 4 feet 10, she could make an outside shot swish through without a sound.

Lusia Harris Stewart (*right*) on the offense

Larry Bird

A Bashful Bird

Larry Bird was homesick. He missed his hometown of French Lick, Indiana. After graduating from high school, Larry went to play for the Hoosiers of Indiana University. The school in Bloomington had a great basketball team and one of the best coaches, Bobby Knight. Larry Bird was happy playing basketball there. But he missed small-town ways. He packed up and moved back home. "It was too big," he said later. Indiana officials were worried. They had hoped their star would go on to great fame. Now Larry Bird was hanging out at the French Lick gas station. His basketball career seemed at an end. Then Larry began to hear from people—from fans, Coach Knight, his mom, even his grandmother. They wanted him to return to college—and basketball. Larry Bird did come back to become one of basketball's finest all-around players. He returned to the campus in the fall of 1975. His skill and determination led him to NBA superstardom. At 6 feet 8 and 200 pounds, Bird had a great long-range jump shot and fingertip "touch." He was Rookie of the Year in 1980 and went on to lead the Boston Celtics to numerous championship titles.

King of the Playground

Crowds gathered to watch at the New York City playground. Everyone wanted to see the kid with the huge hands. He could palm a basketball like it was an orange. He'd pivot on one foot and fly up for a slam-dunk that left the rim humming. It was said that Julius Erving once did an incredible "360" slam-dunk. It swished through, bounced and came up *again* through the bottom of the hoop! Born in 1950, Julius Erving was the king of "playground basketball." On that asphalt surface, toughness counts. So does style. The key is to be able to do it all. Julius once said, "On the playground, you want to outscore your opponent, and you also want to freak him out with a big move or a big block."

Julius Erving was called names like Houdini and the Claw. But Julius was proudest of the nickname that he got in sixth grade. Because he was such a good student, he was called the Doctor. The name followed him through his sports career. In 1971 Dr. J left college to play in the American Basketball Association (ABA). Five years later he was traded to the Philadelphia 76ers, a team he played with for 11 seasons.

Julius "Dr. J" Erving

During that time, he appeared in every All-Star game. He was named the league's MVP in 1981. Spectators marveled at the spins, scoops and jumps that terrified his opponents. Off the court, however, Julius Erving didn't scare anyone. He cared about his fans and worked hard for several charities. Dr. J retired from his sport in 1987. He'll always remain a legend in basketball.

Nancy
Lieberman-Cline

Loving Licorice and Lay-ups

She loves pasta, licorice and basketball. Nancy Lieberman-Cline may be the best female basketball player in the United States. In high school she was one of the first players to be chosen for the 1976 U.S. Olympic basketball team. In 1986 she was the first woman to join a pro league for men, the United States Basketball League. Nancy grew up playing ball with the boys and was accepted on the court as a hard worker. Why would she choose basketball as a career?

Nancy told *Sports Illustrated for Kids*, "When I was about ten, my parents were getting divorced and they would argue all the time. So, just to get out of the house, I would go to play basketball. I got out there and started playing with the guys, and I loved it. I knew then that I wanted to be the best basketball player in the world." And she may be. Look for Nancy Lieberman-Cline in the 1992 Olympics!

Forget the Instant Replay

No one wanted a repeat of the February 2, 1982, game between Chadron (Nebraska) State College and Wayne State. It started when the four officials were 45 minutes late for the tip-off. They had been stopped for speeding and fined $112. Then the national anthem singer forgot the words. Next the karate expert performing the halftime show had troubles. It took him four attempts to hack apart a stack of bricks. Finally Chadron State faltered in the second half. It lost its 17th game of the season, 71-65. The next day a radio announcer told his national audience about the mishaps. He made a boo-boo too. He incorrectly named Con Marshall, sports-information director at Chadron, as the singer who had fumbled the national anthem. It was a game of blunders from beginning to end!

No Pass, No Play

In 1984 the state of Texas passed a "no pass, no play" law. Students earning less than a 70-percent average in any school course could not participate in after-school programs. Some students challenged the law. In 1986 the U.S. Supreme Court let the law stand. Now similar laws are common across the country. Most schools with "no pass, no play" laws offer special programs to help students improve their grades. Coaches are concerned about students who are in danger of failing courses. They don't want to lose their best athletes. Critics of the law say it is not fair to kids. They believe the students need the feeling of success that sports can give them. The law, they maintain, also discourges players from taking tough classes. No pass, no play. What's your opinion?

Hip Hoopsters

The Harlem Globetrotters are the mischief-makers of basketball. These super show-offs play all over the world. They haven't lost a game since 1971. They are court clowns who tease the crowd with their crazy stunts. They hide the ball. They dribble and dazzle with amazing shots.

Organized in 1927, the Globetrotters included only men until 1985. That's when Lynette Woodard joined the team. Three other women have been on the team since then. In 1987 Sandra Gayle Hodge became the fourth woman to join. At 5 feet 8 and 125 pounds, she is small by comparison but mighty. She can make a free throw with her back to the basket! Sandra has performed her dazzling ball-handling tricks to audiences in 50 countries. That's Globetrotting!

Lynette
Woodard

David Johnson (*left*) maneuvers around Patrick Ewing.

It's Never Too Late to Grow Up

David Robinson got a late start in his basketball career. He played only one year of high school basketball. But that didn't slow him down. In his four years at the U.S. Naval Academy in Annapolis, Maryland, David really grew up. In fact, he grew seven inches. He stopped growing at 7 feet 1 inch. David set 33 school records at the academy. He became the first NCAA Division player to score more than 2,500 points, grab more than 1,300 rebounds, and sink more than 60 percent of his shots from the field. He also set NCAA records for most blocked shots in a game (14) and in a season (207). In 1987 David was named top college player of the year. The navy made a special ruling for its tall star. Instead of five years of full-time duty, David would have to serve only two years. The San Antonio Spurs drafted him. The Spurs were willing to wait two years while David served his country.

In 1989 the tallest man in the navy became one of the NBA's top rookies. His very first pro game, in November of 1989, was against the mighty Los Angeles Lakers. David scored 23 points. He had 17 rebounds and blocked one of Magic Johnson's lay-ups. The Spurs upset the Lakers, 106-98. After four straight losing seasons, the Spurs were on their way up—just like their star rookie!

Wake Up to Magic!

Neighbors of young Earvin Johnson Jr. didn't need to set their alarms. They heard the bounce-bounce-bounce of his ball. Magic Johnson would wake up early and head for the schoolyard, dribbling all the way. He would put moves on parked cars as if they were opponents. Sometimes he would have to shovel snow from the basketball court. But now Magic Johnson gets to play in packed arenas all over the country. He has been called one of the modern miracles of basketball.

When Magic left college, the Lakers made him the first pick in the 1979 NBA draft. He has not let them down. Magic has led the Los Angeles team to five NBA championships in ten seasons. He has been the league's Most Valuable Player twice.

Magic grew up with six sisters and three brothers. He shared most of his things—but *not* his basketball. His practice paid off. He has perfected the no-look pass and today makes awesome assists. He is considered the best play-making guard in the NBA.

Now Magic Johnson shares both his talents and his money. Each year he plays in a benefit game that raises about

Magic Johnson tries to pass against Phoenix Suns guard Jay Humphries.

$3 million for the United Negro College Fund. Magic offers this advice to kids: "Set your goals high, practice hard and remember, you are part of a team."

Court Kissing

Isiah Thomas of the Detroit Pistons is one of Magic Johnson's best friends. Millions of TV viewers watched a different kind of opening tip at the 1988-89 NBA finals. It was not the pregame glares of opponents ready to do battle. Instead Magic and Isiah kissed each other on the cheek. Were they embarrassed? "It's just a form of affection," Magic said. "I kiss my dad and my brothers the same way." Isiah and Magic kiss off the comments.

Ribbet, Ribbet

Which basketball team has the worst nickname? Some think there's no question: the Horned Frogs of Texas Christian University. Imagine telling your grandchildren that you were once a Horned Frog!

The Horned Frog, mascot of Texas Christian University

Patrick Ewing holds the ball high.

The Best Center

Who was the best center in the NBA in 1990? The center of attention falls on three candidates: Akeem Olajuwon, Patrick Ewing and David Robinson. Akeem, "the Dream," has led the league in rebounds and blocked shots while scoring 25 points a game. Ewing scored 28 points a game and was fifth in rebounds. Robinson scored 24 points per game and was second in rebounds. Put three fans together and the vote would be close.

Hello—You're on the Air

Talk is cheap. Especially over the radio. Sports talk shows are becoming even more popular in the nineties. Radio talk-show hosts and their callers battle over many sports issues. Coaches, strategies, even the price of a stadium hot dog are debated. Many of the callers become "regulars." They phone almost every night with a sports opinion. Dr. Basketball was a regular caller who knew so much about his sport that he was invited to be a co-host. Now he makes personal appearances wearing fluorescent tights, a cape and a mask! What question would you ask Dr. Basketball? How about "Where do you shop for your clothes?"

Double Good

Kevin Johnson is only the fifth player in NBA history to average more than 20 points and 10 assists per game in a season. Not only that, but he has done it twice! Kevin plays guard for the Phoenix Suns. In the 1988-89 season, Kevin averaged 20.4 points and 12.2 assists. In the 1989-90 season, he averaged 22.5 points and 11.4 assists.

Kevin does good things off the court too. In 1989 he founded St. Hope Academy Youth Center to help kids in Sacramento, California.

Kevin Johnson hangs in the air as he puts up a shot.

44 Forever

Loyola Marymount University had come from behind. Ranked 11th nationally, the Lions had made it to the Final Four in the NCAA tournament. As the team formed a circle on March 8, 1990, they were very sad. They were remembering their teammate Hank Gathers. Only four days earlier Gathers had collapsed on the court and died of heart failure. Some thought the team could not go on. But forward Bo Kimble said of his friend, "Hank would've wanted us to play in the NCAAs."

Hank Gathers had been a sure shooter. It earned him the name Bankman. Number 44 had wanted to remain a big scorer. To keep himself loose, he would shoot free throws left-handed. Teammates honored Gathers's memory. They wrote BANKMAN 44-EVER on the heels of their shoes for the big game.

It was the second half of the Loyola-New Mexico State game that was unforgettable. The teams had been tied at intermission. At the start of the second half Bo Kimble was fouled. Right-handed Kimble took his place at the free-throw line. He shook his left arm just like Hank had done. He took the ball from the ref. Then Kimble calmly released the ball left-handed. It was "in the bank"—for Hank Gathers.

Tall Hair

Kenny Walker, a forward for the New York Knicks, got a new high-rise haircut in 1990. It added four inches to his height. Kenny said, "It makes me taller, and around here they pay by size."

Michael Jordan slams the ball through the hoop.

King of the Courts

Who is the Big Kahuna of basketball? Larry Bird? Magic Johnson? Or how about the Chicago Bulls superstar whose license plate reads FLITE 23? Three-time NBA scoring champion Michael Jordan may get your vote. He performs amazing triple-doubles. He fills the stands. He steals balls. He may be the number one man.

Michael Jordan grew up in Wilmington, North Carolina, with two brothers and two sisters. The family motto was WORK. One family chore was washing the car in the backyard. It was there that Michael's father gave him his special tongue-wagging trademark. He and his father would push out their tongues to concentrate while doing the job. Michael still does the job, but now he WORKS on the opposition. He burns up the court with his high-flying aerial antics. He seems to hang suspended in midair. "Slim, trim and cat-quick" is the way Jordan describes himself.

Michael Jordan became only the third player since Dave Cowens and Larry Bird to lead a team in rebounds, assists, steals and points in the same season. Fans all over the world recognize his genius. Jordan may be the most hounded athlete in all of sports. He signs an average of more than 100 autographs a day.

Michael Jordan is successful in the business world too. What if companies paid athletes in products instead of dollars for their endorsements? Nike would owe Michael Jordan 113,636 pairs of Air Jordan basketball shoes. That would equal his $12.5 million endorsement contract.

Basketball Timelines

1891: James A. Naismith invents the game of basketball.

1892: Rules for basketball are published on January 15 by James Naismith in the YMCA magazine. Soon all the country's YMCAs can adopt the game.

1893: Slightly more than a year after basketball is invented, women are playing too. Smith College is the first women's school to play basketball.

1896: The first college game is played at Iowa City, featuring the University of Chicago against the University of Iowa. The game of basketball is so new that Iowa coach Henry F. Kallenberg has to explain the rules to the nearly 500 fans. Chicago wins, 15-12.

1927: The Harlem Globetrotters is founded.

Billy Ray Hobley of the Harlem Globetrotters

41

1936: Men's basketball is played for the first time as an Olympic sport.

1937: The jump ball after each score is eliminated.

1939: The first NCAA basketball championship game is played. The University of Oregon defeats Ohio State, 46-33.

1940: The first televised basketball game takes place. It is beamed from Madison Square Garden.

1946: The Basketball Association of America (BAA) is founded, with 11 teams in the league. Seven of the franchises from that first season are still playing today. Only two of them, the Boston Celtics and the New York Knicks, remain in business at the same locations.

1949: The Basketball Association of America and the National Basketball League merge to become the National Basketball Association (NBA).

1949: The NBA expands to 17 teams playing a 64-game schedule.

1950: Charles Cooper of Duquesne University in Pittsburgh is the first black drafted into the National Basketball Association.

1950: The Minneapolis Lakers fall to the Fort Wayne Pistons, 19-18. This is the lowest-scoring game in NBA history.

1950: Players may be disqualified from a game by fouling out.

1951: The first NBA All-Star game is played in Boston. East beats West, 111-94.

1954: The 24-second clock is used for the first time in an NBA game.

1959: The Basketball Hall of Fame inducts its first 24 members.

1960: Wilt Chamberlain goes 0 for 10 from the free-throw line—the most free throws attempted without making any in a single game. (Even though he had plenty of practice in his career, the Dipper didn't improve. He was 6,057 of 11,862 from the free-throw line, for an average of .511, an NBA record low.)

1962: On March 2 Wilt "the Stilt" Chamberlain topples records by scoring 100 points in one game. Wilt's Philadelphia Warriors beat the New York Knicks, 169-147.

1967: The American Basketball Association (ABA) begins its first season. George Mikan is its first commissioner.

1968: The Basketball Hall of Fame museum opens in Springfield, Massachusetts.

1969: The Boston Celtics win their 11th NBA championship in 13 years.

1972: John Wooden becomes a double Basketball Hall of Fame honoree. He was elected in the hall's first year (1959) as an outstanding player. Now, in 1972, he is honored as a coach.

1974: Notre Dame breaks UCLA's 88-game winning streak at Notre Dame, 71-70.

1974: Moses Malone signs with the Utah Stars, becoming the first player in modern times to go directly from high school to the pros.

1975: The largest crowd ever watches a women's basketball game. On February 22, more than 11,000 fans come to see the hot match between Queens College and Immaculata College in New York City.

1976: The American Basketball Association folds. Gone are the red, white and blue basketballs and high-flying dunkers.

1976: Women's basketball is included for the first time as an Olympic event.

1978: The Women's Professional Basketball League is formed. It is the first women's pro basketball league.

1979: Ann Meyers becomes the first female to sign a professional basketball contract with the NBA. The four-time UCLA All-American signs a one-year contract for $59,000. She is cut after three days and signs to play with the New Jersey Gems in the Women's Professional Basketball League.

1985: Lynette Woodard becomes the first woman to join the Harlem Globetrotters.

1986: Kareem Abdul-Jabbar adds the fouling crown to his record collection during a game in March. His fourth-quarter personal against Danny Schayes is number 4,194. Asked about his record total, Kareem says, "Yeah, but half of them were bad calls."

1989: The NBA salary cap—the amount of money each team is allowed to spend on players in a year—is set at $9.8 million.

1990: The NBA welcomes two new members for its 44th season. The Orlando Magic and the Minnesota Timberwolves each pay $32.5 million to join. Today's NBA has 27 teams.

1990: Because of the salary-cap rule, the Los Angeles Lakers cannot add to their roster. Magic Johnson makes it possible for the team to afford the asking price of a new player by offering to give up $75,000 of his own salary.

Index